The Unexpected Adventure of FLUFFEN the BEAR

illustrated by Sonja Wimmer

SCHOLASTIC INC.

Written by Morgan Llewellyn. Illustrated by Sonja Wimmer. Designed by Holly Hemphill.

ISBN-13: 978-1-338-28419-5

ISBN-10: 1-338-28419-3

3 4 5 6 7 8 9 10   40   27 26 25 24 23 22 21

Scholastic Inc., 557 Broadway, New York, NY 10012

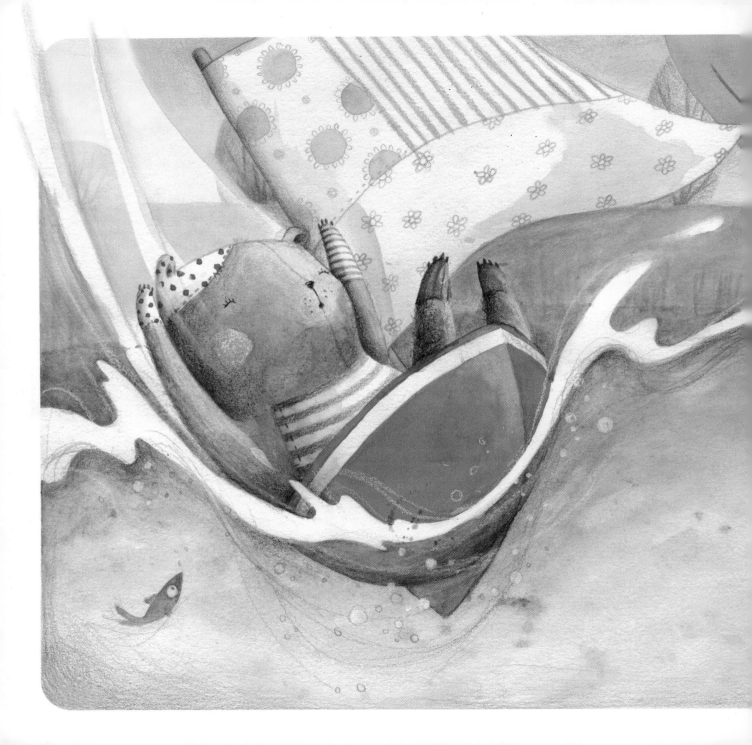

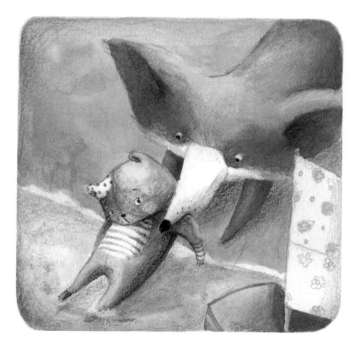

TRY THIS!

Wordless books like this one are perfect for storytelling. Together with your favorite reading partner (child or adult!) tell this story in your own words. Use the tips below to get the most out of your story time.

TELLING FLUFFEN'S STORY

1) **Start slow.** First, go through the book looking at the pictures. Talk about what you both see. Then start again and tell the story together.

2) **Tell it your way.** There is no right or wrong way to "read" a wordless book. Let your imaginations lead the way!

3) **Read it again!** You can "read" this book many ways. Each time you enjoy it together, try focusing on something new:

- **Actions**—Focus on what's happening in the story from beginning to end.

- **Emotions**—Look at the characters' faces. How are they feeling? Why?

- **Details**—Search for all of the details in the background. Where is the story set? Who or what is there?

- **Role Play**—Pretend you are the characters. Give them each a silly voice.

- **Ask Questions**—On each page, ask your reading partner what they notice and think is happening.

ADVENTURE TIME

After you read, extend the adventure with the tips below.

1) **Find a favorite stuffed animal and go on an adventure!** Retell Fluffen's story, or make up a new exciting tale all your own.

   Bonus: Draw pictures of your story and tape them together for your own adventure book!

2) **Go on an outdoor adventure!** Visit your favorite park. Look around and imagine all of the ways that you could have an unexpected journey and…
   Ready, set, go!